CONTENTS

BEHOLD, PARADISE ISLAND!

SILVER BRACELETS

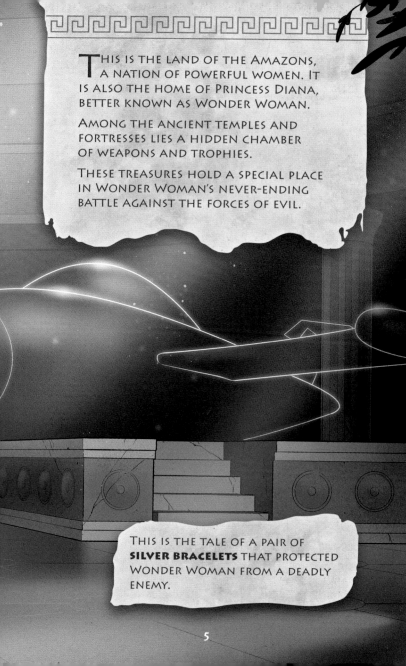

This is the land of the Amazons, a nation of powerful women. It is also the home of Princess Diana, better known as Wonder Woman.

Among the ancient temples and fortresses lies a hidden chamber of weapons and trophies.

These treasures hold a special place in Wonder Woman's never-ending battle against the forces of evil.

This is the tale of a pair of **SILVER BRACELETS** that protected Wonder Woman from a deadly enemy.

CHAPTER 1

LIGHT IN THE JUNGLE

Morning sunlight streams into Wonder Woman's Invisible Jet. The light gleams off her tiara and silver bracelets.

Wonder Woman is flying to Paradise Island. She has been called home by her mother, Queen Hippolyta.

The jet soars over South America. Its powerful engines rumble as it flies above a dense, green jungle.

Suddenly, a blinking light flashes from the trees below.

Wonder Woman looks down at the jungle.

That light looks like a distress signal, she thinks. *Someone must have heard my jet and needs help.*

The jungle is too thick for a plane to land.

Wonder Woman pushes the autopilot button on her controls. Then she lifts the invisible canopy above her seat.

Wonder Woman leaps out of the jet and flies into the wind.

SSWOOOSHHHH!

She soars down to a small clearing in the jungle.

Wonder Woman kneels in the clearing. She looks down and sees a hand mirror.

"Someone signalled me with this mirror by reflecting sunlight," she says. "But where are they now?"

HEEELLLPPPP!

A scream rips through the air.

CHAPTER 2

A VILLAIN WITH CLAWS

Wonder Woman turns and sees a camp near the trees. A feline figure stands next to a tent.

Cheetah! thinks Wonder Woman.

The villain is pulling a young woman towards a big animal cage.

"Try living in a cage," snarls Cheetah. "Like the poor animals you trap."

"I'm a scientist, and I love animals!" says the woman. "I only trap them to do quick medical check-ups. Then I let them go."

"Release her," orders Wonder Woman as she strides towards her old enemy.

"Wonder Woman!" cries Cheetah.

The villain pounces at Wonder Woman with outstretched arms. Her deadly talons flash in the sunlight.

Wonder Woman raises her bracelets to block the attack.

SHING! SHING!

Sparks fly! Cheetah's sharp claws are useless against Wonder Woman's unbreakable bracelets.

"My claws can't break your bracelets," says Cheetah, "but I think I know what might!"

The villain flees into the jungle. Wonder Woman swiftly chases her.

CHAPTER 3

STEEL JAWS

"You're on my turf now," Cheetah calls out, running far ahead of Wonder Woman. "And I have a few surprises for you!"

Wonder Woman races through the jungle.

CLICK!

She hears the sound of metal. Then the jaws of a giant animal trap spring up around her.

Wonder Woman quickly sweeps her hands upwards.

KA-TANNGGG!

The silver bracelets catch the jaws, stopping them from closing.

But the trap is powered by giant springs.
The jaws keep pressing closer and closer.

Sweat rolls down Wonder Woman's face. She
strains against the metal teeth.

"Hera, help me!" Wonder Woman cries.

With a burst of strength, Wonder Woman thrusts her arms outwards.

KRAAAACKKKKKKK!

The bracelets shatter the trap!

GRRRRRRR!

Cheetah growls.

"That was only the first trap!" says the villain. "Let's see if you can get out of the next one!"

Cheetah flees once more. Wonder Woman rushes after her.

CHAPTER 4

A THOUSAND ARROWS

Deep in the jungle, Cheetah stops. She turns to face Wonder Woman.

As Wonder Woman draws closer, the ground under her feet gives way.

Wonder Woman tumbles into a deep pit. Mechanical bows armed with arrows surround her.

"I've dipped each arrow in poison," Cheetah shouts down. "Bye-bye, Wonder Woman!"

Wonder Woman tenses her muscles.

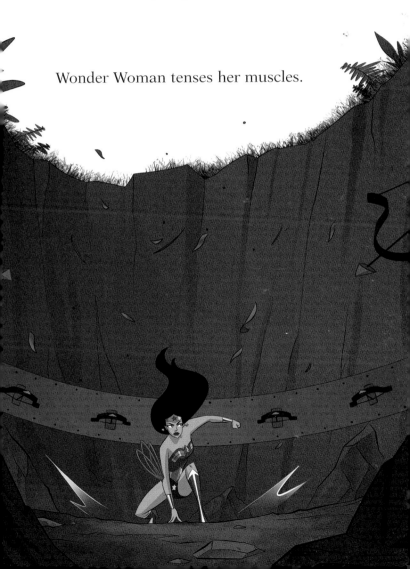

She takes a deep breath.

FFFFT! FFFFT! FFFFT!

The arrows spring from the bows.

Wonder Woman raises her silver bracelets and spins like a top.

CLINK! CLINK! CLINK!

The arrows bounce off the bracelets as Wonder Woman twirls faster and faster.

Soon, piles of broken arrows lie harmlessly around her.

"Cheetah!" Wonder Woman shouts as she comes to a stop. "Is that all you've got?"

AAAAHHHH!

Wonder Woman's super-hearing picks up a distant scream.

Cheetah is back at that camp, she thinks.

CHAPTER 5

SHINING SILVER

Wonder Woman leaps out of the pit and flies back to the camp.

The scientist is trapped inside an animal cage. And the cage has been loaded onto a raft.

Cheetah is nowhere in sight.

Wonder Woman rushes towards the raft to free the woman.

"Wonder Woman, look out!" warns the scientist.

Wonder Woman spins and sees Cheetah. The villain holds a blowpipe.

Wonder Woman knows blowpipes fire poison darts. One powerful breath will send the dart straight at her.

Cheetah aims the blowpipe and takes a deep breath.

Wonder Woman raises her arms. She catches the gleaming sunlight on her silver bracelets.

"Yiiii!" Cheetah screams. Bright sunlight reflects into her catlike eyes.

The blinded villain lowers the blowpipe for one second. That's all Wonder Woman needs.

Wonder Woman hurls her golden lasso and snags the villain in a tight loop. Then she frees the scientist.

"Thank you, Wonder Woman!" the scientist says with a sigh of relief.

"I should thank you," says Wonder Woman with a smile. "Your signal with the mirror gave me the idea to blind Cheetah."

Wonder Woman glances at her snarling, struggling foe.

"After spending some time in prison," says Wonder Woman, "perhaps Cheetah will finally see the light!"

GLOSSARY

autopilot device that keeps an aircraft flying on a set course without a pilot

blowpipe weapon that uses the force of someone's breath to shoot an arrow or dart

canopy sliding cover over the cockpit of a small plane

distress signal call for help

feline having to do with any animal of the cat family

mechanical having to do with machines or tools

medical having to do with medicine

poison substance that can kill or harm someone

talon long, sharp claw

turf someone's personal territory

villain wicked or evil character in a story

DISCUSS

1. Why does Cheetah want to lock up the scientist? Is she right or wrong to do so? Discuss your reasons.

2. Wonder Woman uses her silver bracelets to fight off many of Cheetah's attacks and traps. Why are they the best tool for her to use in this story?

3. Cheetah uses her catlike powers and abilities to battle Wonder Woman. If you could have the power of any animal, which would you choose and why?

WRITE

1. Imagine you are the scientist in this story. Write a diary or journal entry that explains what happened from your point of view.

2. If you had a powerful piece of jewellery like Wonder Woman's silver bracelets, what would it be? Write a short paragraph describing what your piece of jewellery would do and draw a picture of it.

3. At the end of the story, Wonder Woman captures Cheetah. Write the next chapter showing their trip to prison. Does Wonder Woman get her there safely or does the villain escape? You decide!

AUTHOR

Michael Dahl is the author of more than 200 books for children and young adults, including *Bedtime for Batman*, *Be A Star, Wonder Woman!* and *Sweet Dreams, Supergirl*. He has won the AEP Distinguished Achievement Award three times for his non-fiction, a Teachers' Choice Award from *Learning* magazine and a Seal of Excellence from the Creative Child Awards. He is also the author of the Batman Tales of the Batcave and Superman Tales of the Fortress of Solitude series. Dahl currently lives in Minnesota, USA.

ILLUSTRATOR

Omar Lozano lives in Monterrey, Mexico. He has always been crazy about illustration and is constantly on the lookout for awesome things to draw. In his free time, he watches lots of films, reads fantasy and sci-fi books, and draws! Omar has worked for Marvel, DC, IDW, Capstone and several other publishers.